Jane Blonde
the perfect spylet

JILL MARSHALL

MAC...KS

First published 2008 by Macmillan Children's Books
a division of Macmillan Publishers Limited
20 New Wharf Road, London N1 9RR
Basingstoke and Oxford
www.panmacmillan.com

Associated companies throughout the world

ISBN 978-0-330-45680-7

1 3 5 7 9 8 6 4 2

A CIP catalogue record for this book is available from
the British Library.

Typeset by Nigel Hazle
Printed and bound in Great Britain by Mackays of Chatham plc, Kent

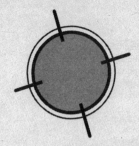

for perfect spylets everywhere

Jane Blonde, Sensational Spylet – who just minutes ago had been ordinary schoolgirl Janey Brown – emerged from the Wower in her trademark silver Lycra SPIsuit. The fabulous spy shower had transformed her, once more, into a shimmering picture of Spylet perfection. Her multifunctional platinum ponytail danced from side to side, and her keen eyes sparkled behind her slender Ultra-gog glasses. Everything was as normal for the country's number-one girl-spy-in-training. Except—

'Bent bananas!' G-Mamma shuddered as Blonde hobbled across the Spylab. 'You look like you need a walking stick. What is *wrong* with the Blonde?'

Janey shrugged – or at least tried to. 'It feels

1

a bit . . .' She wriggled and dropped into a couple of combat poses, '. . . tight.'

Her SPI:KE (Solomon's Polificational Investigations: Kid Educator) slapped a hand to her forehead, wincing as she caught herself in the eye with a large diamanté cocktail ring. 'You've had a growth spurt!'

'I think I must have,' said Janey. 'My toes are crammed up against the end of my Fleet-feet. Shall we try and stretch it a bit?'

'Won't work, Bendy Blondey.' G-Mamma shook her head, a terrifying gleam in her eye. 'No, there's nothing else for it.'

Janey stepped back in alarm as G-Mamma lunged towards her, brandishing a small square of plastic. 'What are you going to with that?!'

'With *this*, girly-girl, I'm taking you shopping.' G-Mamma waved the plastic card around gleefully. 'It just arrived from your dad. Unlimited spending on a Sol's Spredit Account – that's way-hey. We've got the money, honey.'

Janey grinned. Her father was the mysterious head of Solomon's Polificational Investigations. His work as a global spying genius kept him pretty busy, but he always looked after Janey from a distance, in whatever ways he could.

'Well, tomorrow's Saturday. I'm meant to be going round to see Alfie, but he won't mind if I cancel to go shopping.' Janey couldn't really imagine that Alfie Halliday, her best friend and fellow Spylet, would want to accompany her and her SPI:KE on a shopping trip.

But G-Mamma was already wrapping Trouble the Spycat around her neck like a fat furry scarf and tugging on her crimson roller boots. 'Pah! Forget tomorrow. Do you think spy shops open so any old boring ordinaries can go in? Blonde-girl, we're going right now. Shopping for spy-goods is a night-time activity – you'll see. Now grab your ASPIC.'

'But it's midnight . . .' started Janey, but G-Mamma had already zoomed downstairs to her front door and Trouble was miaowing for Janey to follow. She rolled her eyes. Her mum had tucked her up in bed four hours ago – little did she know that, minutes later, Janey had zipped through the spy-door that linked her bedroom to G-Mamma's Spylab next door.

Janey sighed. Here we go again, she thought . . .

They careered down back streets at break-neck speed – Janey on her Aeronautical SPI Conveyor, G-Mamma on her super-fast SPIskates. After a while Janey realized that they were headed for the city's main shopping district, where she and her mum came to do their Christmas shopping. Moments later they were on Cambridge Street, where all the biggest shops were. They slowed to a less conspicuous pace so as not to draw too much attention from passers-by.

Janey looked around her. 'But these are just ordinary shops.'

'Ha! They're mostly pretty boring, I'll grant you,' said G-Mamma, cruising to a halt in front of Janey's mum's favourite department store. 'but Seacrest and Argents is just a little special. Follow me, Zany Janey, into . . . wonderland!'

'G-Mamma, I think you're wrong,' hissed Janey as her SPI:KE looked around to make sure no one was watching then swiped her Spredit card down the door frame.

G-Mamma snorted. 'Am I now?' she said as

the door evaporated before them. 'Watch and learn, Spylet. Watch. And. Learn . . .'

Janey gasped as, tingling with anticipation, she followed G-Mamma into the dark department store. What if the alarm went off? She imagined trying to explain to the police that she was just looking for a new SPIsuit . . . at one o'clock in the morning. They'd think she was crazy! She pointed to the swanky make-up and perfume counters. 'Are you *sure* this is a special spy store?'

'Seacrest and Argents, Blondelicious. Think about it.' G-Mamma skidded towards the 'up' escalator. 'Just lose a few little letters and you've got "secret agents"! Clever huh? Welcome to SPI's very own department store. Yup, your daddykins owns this place. And tonight, Zany Janey, it's all just for us.'

Janey glanced around her. SPI's very own store? But there was no time to question G-Mamma any further as the SPI:KE was halfway up the escalator.

'Come on, Blondey,' she called. 'Children's Wear is up here.'

Janey pulled herself together and stepped

5

on to the escalator. Once she reached the top G-Mamma spun round with a flourish.

'Here we are,' she crooned. 'We'll get everything you need here.'

'Where?' said Janey. Surely her new Blonde outfit wasn't going to be jeans and a jumper?

G-Mamma's glitter-dusted eyes gleamed. 'Now, I just need to activate the sprinklers . . .'

'The sprinklers? What?! Nooo, G-Mamma, nooooooooooooo!'

G-Mamma had many moments of madness, but this one seemed spectacularly enormous, the mad moment to end all mad moments. Suddenly she grabbed Janey's hand and trained the laser finger of her Girl-gauntlet gadget-glove at a sprinkler on the ceiling. Then the SPI:KE squeezed hard. Janey tried in vain to free her hand, and cringed as within seconds the sprinkler system sprang into action. Everything was getting soaked! Janey shook her head in despair. G-Mamma had finally lost it.

But then the SPI:KE abruptly let go of Janey's hand and spread her arms wide. 'A rap to mark the occasion.' She shimmied and swayed, cobra-like, in front of Janey.

'Seacrest and Argents is the place to buy
Every little thing you need to spy:
Gauntlets, ASPICs, LipSPICKs, Gogs,
Fleet-feet, SPIsuits and SPI-Pods.
Every single piece of Spylet gear
Is here – at – S&A. Oh yeah!'

G-Mamma finished with a deafening whoop.
'I was thinking of recording that one. What do
you think?'

Janey was too busy staring to answer. The
sprinkler system had stopped, and while G-
Mamma had been rapping, something quite
amazing had happened. The rails of regular
children's clothes were now laden with SPIsuits
of every colour, size and design imaginable. She
could see her own silver suit and the soft silky
denim-look one that Alfie wore when he transformed into Spylet Al Halo. To the left and right
were piles of accessories – Girl-gauntlets and
Boy-battlers, racks of Ultra-gogs in a range of
frames and colours, Fleet-feet, Fleet-boots,
eSPIdrills, Rollerblades, rocket hairclips, chunky
necklaces that Janey knew were SPIVs (SPI
Visualators) . . .

She turned around slowly. 'It's incredible! Not your rap . . . I mean, that's very good, obviously,' Janey added quickly, 'but this *place* . . . It's . . . I : . . how . . . ?'

'You work it out, Blonde, like a good little Spylet.' G-Mamma folded her arms and waited.

And with the small flash in her brain that always accompanied a moment of Spylet understanding, it came to Janey. 'It's a giant Wower. The sprinklers changed the clothes and stuff like the one in the Spylab changes me.'

'Bingo!' said G-Mamma with a grin. 'The Power of the Wower, girly-girl. And now, finally, we can get on with some shopping.'

They spent a very happy hour foraging through the rails, and Janey settled on one that was exactly like her original silver SPIsuit. She staggered round the Children's Wear department, laden with SPIVs, new white boots with Fleet-feet soles, plus a whole selection of spy jewellery. G-Mamma disappeared for a few minutes and returned with a neat peaked cap in Janey's school colours. 'Just picked this up from "Special Orders". I sent the manufacturing

8

team a regular Winton School cap and they've customized it.'

'G-Mamma, I can't wear that – I'd get laughed out of class.' Janey tried to topple it off the pile.

'But it's a PERSPIRE – Personal SPI Remote Educator.'

'Er, right. Nice name,' said Janey, wrinkling her nose.

'It's a computer – look.' G-Mamma pressed the tiny bobble on the top and flipped the cap over. 'A laser-light keyboard and screen, both invisible until activated. It's got a motherboard the size of an ant tucked in under the bobble, but it can do everything my Spylab computer can do.'

Janey shook her head firmly. 'No way. Only the tiny first years ever wear school caps.'

'As you wish, JB . . . Right, I'm going over to the women's department to pick myself up a few things.'

G-Mamma led the way, Rollerblading to the women's ranges. 'These are no good. Too small. I need the "For Spies Who Like Pies range".'

Pretty soon she was twirling and gyrating in front of a 360-degree mirror. Janey, bored, decided to take a look around. She rode the escalators down to the ground floor and made for the huge Food Hall at the back. Trouble trotted along at her heels. The Food Hall hadn't been Wowed – and Janey thought she'd better not set the sprinklers off when G-Mamma wasn't around. But as she stopped to gawp at a display of old-fashioned gobstoppers, she wondered whether if you ate them they would be transformed into explosive SPInamite, like the special sweets that sometimes formed part of her spygear kit. After a few minutes browsing the foodie treats Janey found herself at the back of the store, near a set of closed double doors.

Suddenly Trouble started to arch his back and spit furiously. 'What's up, Twubs?' asked Janey, bending down to comfort him. The cat began to frantically paw at the doors. He's trying to tell me something, thought Janey. Puzzled, she unbolted the doors. They led outdoors to a delivery area, and as Janey stepped through them she got a mighty shock. Something feathered was flapping around her head! Was it attacking her? Janey put her hands up to defend herself, but the bird fell to the ground and lay there squawking pitifully. 'Oh dear, you poor thing, you're injured. Now Trouble, will you stop that miaowing?' Janey scolded as she bent down to take a closer look.

A bright black button of an eye winked up at her through the semi-darkness, as if simply to say *Help*.

Janey's heart melted. 'Hello, little magpie,' she said softly. The gleaming black and white head tipped on one side and the bird hopped on to Janey's arm. 'Oh, you've hurt your wing. Well, don't worry – I'll fix you up. You must have been feeling so alone out here.'

Trouble gave a yowl that suggested that if the magpie was feeling all alone, it could actually be tucked away cosily – inside his stomach. 'Trouble, stop that. We're taking little Maggie home.' The magpie cocked her head again, and Janey could swear that she understood every word. The bird was lovely. And lonely, just as Janey herself used to be, before she found her SPI friends.

Janey found G-Mamma at Counter

Intelligence, where all goods could be paid for with a swipe of the Spredit card.

But when G-Mamma caught sight of Maggie, she was less than impressed. 'Whoa there, Blondie Baby, where did you find *that*? A bashed-up birdie wasn't on the shopping list, from what *I* remember . . .'

Janey pleaded with her SPI:KE to let her take the bird back to the Spylab, so it could be fixed up in the Wower. Eventually she managed to win her round, but G-Mamma was still grumbling about feathers and sneezing fits as a set of robotic hands appeared to neatly wrap their purchases. Then Jane Blonde and G-Mamma (sporting a floral PERSPIRE cap and a red crystal SPIV the size of a cricket ball) slid out of Seacrest and Argents into the twilight, with a bundle of new SPI-buys strapped on to a new-model magenta ASPIC. The rather startled-looking magpie was perched on the top like the cherry on a cake, and Trouble slunk along behind, somewhat put out.

perfect prefects

'You do know what magpies are famous for?' said Alfie as they walked into school on Monday morning.

'Do they talk?' said Janey excitedly. 'I'm sure she can understand me.'

Alfie tutted. 'That's mynah birds. No, they don't talk. They steal.'

'Oh.' That explained quite a bit. G-Mamma had turned out to be a brilliant bird-nurse, but she had spent rather a lot of time asking Janey where she'd put this or that new trinket. I'll check Maggie's cage when I get back to the lab, thought Janey.

'Oop. Mother alert,' said Alfie, taking off down the side path in an attempt to avoid Mrs Halliday: his mother, headmistress of Winton School, and superSPI.

'I've seen you already, Alfie. Don't bother trying to disappear. Good morning, Janey.' She smiled amiably. 'Glad I found you together. Mr Peters called in sick, so I'm supposed to be looking after the reception class this morning, but Janey's godmother has just received something from SPI headquarters that I really must attend to.'

'We'll check it out for you,' said Alfie quickly, knowing that a message from Janey's father usually marked the beginning of an exciting new adventure.

'Thank you, I'll do that myself.' Mrs Halliday pointed towards the mobile classroom that housed the reception class. 'But the class specifically asked if you'd keep an eye on them, Janey. Seems you're quite a hero to the receptioners! It's just for ten minutes or so.'

Janey was flattered that the little ones had asked for her – she tried to be nice to all the new pupils as she knew how hard it was to start a school and have no friends.

Alfie was less keen. He groaned. 'Babysitting? Aw, Mum.'

'No, not *babysitting*, Alfie Halliday. I call it Acting Your Age and Being Responsible.'

She handed them each a badge. Alfie read it upside down. 'Perfect,' he said. 'Thanks, Mum, but I don't think *that* will go down too well with the other kids.'

'It says "Prefect", you twit,' said Janey.

Mrs Halliday smiled. 'You don't mind, Janey, do you?'

Of course Janey would far rather have been investigating her father's message, but unlike Alfie she knew better than to cross the fierce but fair headmistress. And anyway, the little ones *had* asked for her. 'It's just for a while, though, Mrs H.? I don't have much experience with little kids.'

Mrs Halliday winked as she swung through the door. 'Oh, I don't know about that, Janey. You spend enough time with Alfie.'

As Janey and Alfie climbed up the steps of the mobile classroom, they could hear that the place was in chaos. Janey opened the door to find the dozen receptioners either crying, fighting or bouncing around with their hand up because they needed the toilet. In at least one case it appeared they were too late – a dark stain was spreading down the leg of one pair of brand-new trousers. All the littlies were trussed up in too-big uniforms, including the ridiculous school cap that Janey had spurned.

Janey coughed politely, but the noise level remained the same. 'Everybody,' she said gently, 'let's calm down. Come and sit here, please.'

Nothing.

'BE QUIET, ALL OF YOU!' yelled Alfie. But that obviously wasn't the way to go either. In fact, it made matters even worse as ten of the twelve children started to wail. 'Good grief,' he said. 'It's catching.'

Only one child appeared unworried by it all. She was by the bookcase, flicking through a picture book, her hazel eyes bright and owl-like behind her round metal-rimmed glasses. When the sound of sobbing made her look up, she picked up her book, flicked a ginger plait over her shoulder and walked over to Janey.

'Tell them you'll read them a story,' she said. 'This is a good one. And tell them you're the teacher.'

'I'm not . . . I mean . . .' Janey took the book from her. 'Thank you. Er, class, I'm *Miss* Janey today.'

'I'm Cassie,' said the little girl solemnly. Then she sat down on the nearest cushion and nodded at the picture book.

'Right,' said Janey. 'Everyone, could you get comfy on a cushion, and I'll read you a story.'

But there was no response.

'Story time!' she called in a sing-song voice.

Again nothing. Alfie shrugged.

Cassie blinked at them and then suddenly she clapped out a rhythm. Instantly the children stopped what they were doing, dropped to the cushions and clapped the same rhythm back to her. Janey almost laughed. 'Clapping classes,' she whispered to Alfie. 'G-Mamma would love this.'

'Miss Janey's going to read "The Snuffle-bug" to us,' said Cassie firmly.

'Yay,' cried one little girl, snot oozing down her face. 'My favourite!'

Janey could hardly believe it. As she began to read they were transformed into little angels, each one of them, hanging on to her every word and joining in with the chorus. Before too long she was actually enjoying herself, jumping off her chair to do monster actions as Alfie studied his shoelaces, trying to pretend he wasn't there.

17

Just as she was turning back to start the story of the Snufflebug for the third time, the door opened and Mrs Halliday appeared. 'Ah, well done. All under control, I see. Alfie, you'll have to take over reading the book for a moment. I need Janey's help.'

'What?!' Alfie looked as though he might be sick. 'You've got to be kidding.'

Janey handed him the book. 'Have fun . . .' she said with a grin, before shooting off after his mother.

'We need your code-cracking skills, Janey,' said the headmistress as she marched briskly into her office. 'The message, as ever, isn't terribly clear to us. May I have my seat back, Rosie?'

G-Mamma looked up with a guilty expression. She had been spinning round on the leather chair, which was now a good ten inches lower than it had been before. She wound it up carefully and sat down next to Janey. 'As usual, the mystic cryptic's confused us all.'

There was a shoebox on the desk between them, and Janey felt a little surge of excitement in her stomach. Her father always sent very special things in shoeboxes: gadgets, clues about mission, warnings . . .

G-Mamma took the lid off, and Janey reached over and took three items out of the box, one by one.

First there was a cuddly toy bee, the type that might be tied over a baby's cot. Under that was a map. Janey opened it up across the desk, to find that it was a map of an area she had never heard of. But, more surprisingly, it was covered with drawn-on question marks. The final item was the biggest surprise of all.

'Mince pies?' exclaimed Janey, pulling out a red-ribboned box of pastries. She frowned. 'It isn't Christmas for ages.'

'Exactly,' said G-Mamma. 'Highly irregular. So what do you reckon, Jane the Brain?'

Janey was on the edge of her seat. She loved solving puzzles like this. She just had to think things through slowly and logically. Every item was in the box for a reason, and the hidden message was something her father wanted her to work out. 'Well,' she said, 'there's a bee, and a map. Bee. Map. But what are the question marks for? And where exactly is this?' Suddenly she looked up triumphantly. 'That's it!'

'Good,' said Mrs Halliday, nodding encouragingly. 'What?'

'Not *what* is it. *Where* is it? That's all that's important. *Where.*' She lifted up the bee and then the map in turn. 'Bee. Where. Bee. Where.'

'Spot the bee?' G-Mamma bobbed up and down on her seat. 'Sounds like a fun game.'

'No, "bee where" means BEWARE.'

'Aha! I see!' said Mrs Halliday. 'Beware of what?'

But this was as far as Janey had got. She held up the red-ribboned box. 'Beware the . . . er . . . mince pies?' She shrugged. 'It's all I can think of.'

G-Mamma's eyes grew rounder than ever. 'It's me! They're targeting me. Someone's poisoned all the mince pies in the country, knowing I'm bound to eat one some day.'

'I'm not sure that's it,' said Mrs Halliday after staring at G-Mamma for a long moment.

'Just to be sure,' said G-Mamma, ripping the lid off the box, 'I'll test each one of these. I'll do it for my country,' she said bravely.

Janey reached over and removed the pie from G-Mamma's grasp. 'If Dad says we have to be careful about them, then I think we should take it seriously. So – who stocks mince pies when it's not Christmas?'

'Good thinking.' Mrs Halliday nodded to G-Mamma. 'Rosie, you go and run some tests on these pies. Try not to eat the evidence. I'll do some research here, see who might have them in stock.'

'What should I do?' Janey was ready to put SPI work before schoolwork.

But at that moment the decision was taken out of their hands. Alfie's scarlet face appeared around the door and he ushered in the little boy with the stain on his trousers. 'Um, there's a bit of an emergency.'

Mrs Halliday sighed. 'Alfie, if one of them needed the toilet you should have just taken him.'

'One of them did,' he said. 'That's not the emergency. But when I got back to the class-room, all the rest of them had ... um ... disappeared.'

Mrs Halliday toppled her chair over in

her haste to get out of the room, and Janey ran after the two Halos as they pelted towards the classroom. Had some evil spy organization kidnapped a whole class of little children? So much for 'perfect'. She and Alfie had to be the worst prefects of all time.

3 mincer pincers

Janey was the first to spot them, carrying their cushions over to the wooded area at the edge of the playing field. Cassie was in the lead, her little legs stomping determinedly over tree roots and lost tennis balls.

'Cassie!' Panting, Janey sped across the field, wishing that she was wearing her Fleet-feet. 'Wait! Where are you going?'

Finally she got their attention, and first Cassie and then the whole class, except the one little boy who was still trailing around after Alfie, spun round to look at her. 'Hello, Miss Janey,' Cassie squeaked.

Janey brushed her hair off her sticky fore-head. 'What are you all doing? You can't go wandering off on your own.'

23

Two or three of the children realized they were in trouble, and their faces crumpled. 'But we wanted to do the Snufflebug actions out in the wood, where the Snufflebug does them,' said Cassie.

She looked so disappointed, and the others so forlorn and innocent, that Janey couldn't bear to let them down. 'All right,' she said. 'Quickly. And then I'll take you right back to the classroom. Mrs Halliday is very worried about you.'

Cassie beamed a gappy grin and chanted, 'Snufflebug! Snufflebug!'

'Snufflebug! Snufflebug!' chorused the other children, jumping up and down.

'One minute only,' warned Janey as she crouched down low under the trees. The children all copied her.

Janey began. 'The Snufflebug started as small as a . . .'

'Nut!' screamed the children, folding themselves into the smallest, roundest shapes they could.

'And grew like a daisy, so tall, so strong.' Janey unfurled her slender frame, watching as the children did the same.

'Until he could reach the top of the . . .'

'Hut!'

'Just like the big bug he'd been all along.' As the last words left her mouth, the children joining in with shouts of delight and laughter, Janey threw her arms over her head and leaped up in the air.

And suddenly everything went dark . . .

Janey came to with twelve worried little faces peering down at her, and two bigger, even more worried ones looming above them.

'Janey, what on earth happened?' said Mrs Halliday. 'You've got a bump the size of an egg.'

Janey sat up groggily and touched her head. 'Ow. I was being the Snufflebug,' she said. 'I jumped up and then . . . I don't know.'

'You hit your head on that low branch,' said Cassie earnestly.

'Yeah, you went BANG and fell down SPLAT!' yelled a small boy. 'It was funny!'

'It was dangerous,' said Mrs Halliday sternly. 'Janey could have been seriously hurt. And as for you, reception,' she said, turning to the

25

onlookers, 'who said you could leave the class-room?'

'Cassie said,' shouted one of the boys. 'She—' But then he suddenly fell quiet and hung his head.

'We just wanted to be Snufflebugs,' said Cassie, frowning.

'Well, you can't be Snufflebugs whenever it pleases you. Let's get you all back to the class-room, and Janey, we'll get that head seen to.'

'With vinegar and brown paper?' Alfie snig-gered, but Janey could still see that he was quite worried – whether about her, or about what punishment he might receive for losing a class, she didn't know.

'I'll be fine,' she said. 'Just need to sit down.'

They made their way back to the recep-tion hut, where two of the children pulled up the teacher's chair for her. 'Sorry, Miss Janey,' they chorused, and she patted their chubby little hands gratefully.

'I'll take over from here,' said Mrs Hal-liday firmly. 'Alfie, would you call Janey's mother . . .'

'*God*mother,' said Janey. If her mum got all worried about her, she'd keep Janey on a tighter rein. With the promise of a new mission in the air, Janey had to be ready to act.

'Very well, Janey – your godmother – she should be home by now. Go with Alfie. And class, we're going to work on our alphabet.'

Alfie grabbed Janey by the elbow and steered her down the steps of the classroom. 'Let's call G-Mamma.'

'No need,' said Janey, reaching for the SPIV that was carefully hidden under her navy school jumper. As soon as they were out of sight she spoke into it urgently. 'G-Mamma, are you there?'

Her SPI:KE's face popped into view. She appeared to have developed a mole on her top lip, but Janey quickly realized it was a currant. 'You're not meant to be eating those mince pies!'

'It's a *scientific* test,' said G-Mamma, swallowing quickly. 'Now, waddya want? Chop chop.' There were probably still some pies to get through, and G-Mamma didn't seem to appreciate the interruption.

'I've bumped my head, and Mrs H. said I ought to have it checked out.'

'What bumped you?' G-Mamma's face perked up with interest. 'Something to do with your dad's warning, do you think?'

'No, I just jumped and, um, hit a branch. It was my fault. So will you come and pick me up?'

'There in five, spies alive.' There was a rustling sound – grabbing a pie for the journey, thought Janey – then G-Mamma's face disappeared from view.

Alfie walked with Janey to the gate. 'It's not my fault, whatever Mum thinks. That boy needed to go to the loo, so I had to go too.'

'I thought he'd already, you know, been,' said Janey, thinking of the damp patch on his little uniform trousers.

'So did I, but he's only little, isn't he? He got this really weird look in his eye and said he had to go straight away, so I didn't want to take the risk.' He waved down the street as G-Mamma's car turned the corner. 'I tell you what: if Mum ever asks me to do something like that again, I'm resigning.'

'As a Spylet?'

'No, as her son.'

Janey grinned as she clambered into the passenger seat, though even that made her wince. G-Mamma took one look at her face and turned pale. 'Lumps and bumps! You look like you're growing a new head.'

'Maybe a new one would hurt less than this one,' said Janey, as she waved goodbye to Alfie.

'I'll come into the Spylab and have a Wower,' she said, leaning her aching skull against the headrest. It was not just the pain she wanted to get rid of; hopefully the Wower would eliminate her sense of shame that Jane Blonde, Sensational Spylet, had managed to knock herself out impersonating the Snufflebug.

As she stood under the pearlescent droplets of the spy shower, feeling the bump on her forehead melting away and her body being encased in silver Lycra, Janey could hear G-Mamma pottering around in the lab. 'If you've lost something, check Maggie's cage,' she shouted over the intercom. 'Alfie says they're thieves.'

There was a loud clatter and an insulted

squawk and then G-Mamma exclaimed delight-edly, 'Burgled baubles, you're right! Well, who's a clever little magpie then? Yes, she is. Oh, yes she is. Ow!' shrieked G-Mamma.

'Did she peck you?' Janey stepped into the lab, sensational in her Jane Blonde outfit.

'Not her – that blessed cat scratched me.' G-Mamma rubbed her ankle. 'You are such a jealous kitty, Trouble. Any more scratching like that and you'll never be Wowed again.'

Trouble shifted sulkily. Unusually for a cat, he absolutely loved water and took any oppor-tunity he could to Wow up into his spy-cat self: a glowing golden-tailed beast with hypnotic em-erald eyes and a special sabre-claw like a pirate's cutlass. Janey stroked his head – she couldn't really blame him for getting a bit jealous about all the attention Maggie had been getting. 'You're still number one, Twubs,' she whispered, and he rubbed his head against her hand.

'Blonde!' said G-Mamma. 'Incoming mes-sage.' Janey turned to look at the large plasma screen that dominated one wall of the Spylab. It was crackling into life, and suddenly a very large Mrs Halliday appeared.

'Janey, you look much better. I take it you've been Wowed. Well, I'm glad you're back on form. I've got something to show you.' Mrs Halliday held up a piece of paper. 'I've done that research on year-round mince pies. And you'll never guess which shop has them in stock right now . . .'

Janey knew even before Mrs Halliday could finish her sentence. 'Seacrest and Argents?'

'Well, it's about time we got to the heart of this pesky pie plot.' G-Mamma's eyes gleamed. 'Blonde, we're going shopping again.'

'Good idea,' said Mrs Halliday from the screen. 'And after that, if I could ask you the most enormous favour, Janey – it's just that you were so popular with the reception class that they've asked for you again. They've got pet hour after lunch, and two of the children are bringing in their pets. It would be so great if you could just watch them for a bit – their teacher's still off sick.'

It wasn't exactly high spying, but Janey didn't feel she could refuse. 'OK,' she said eventually. 'I'll bring Trouble too!'

'Marvellous,' beamed Mrs Halliday gratefully. 'Back here at one thirty.'

One thirty, thought Janey. That gives me precisely thirty-two minutes to infiltrate Sea-crest and Argents in the middle of the day, investigate their mince-pie stock and get to school with my spy-pet. She hauled her school jumper and skirt over her Spysuit. 'Trouble, you meet me at the reception classroom at one twenty-five.'

Maggie let out an outraged squawk as if to say *What about me? Can't I come?* She fixed Janey with a baleful stare.

'I'm sorry, Maggie, but you're not well enough to come. Maybe next time.'

Maggie ruffled her tail feathers huffily, but Janey didn't have time to soothe her now. 'Come on, G-Mamma. We have to go.'

They sped to Seacrest and Argents in G-Mamma's car, parked on a double yellow line and dashed through the revolving doors into the store. This time the Food Hall was bustling with people.

'I'll check the cakes and biscuits,' said Janey, steering G-Mamma past a display of multicoloured doughnuts. Sending her to the confectionary section would be far too dangerous. 'You could, er, check they're not, um, elsewhere?'

G-Mamma tottered off a little sulkily, and Janey made for the baked-goods section near the back of the shop.

'Right . . . jam tarts. No. Apple tarts. Cupcakes. No, no, no.'

Then suddenly she noticed a pile of redribboned boxes leaning drunkenly against a large pillar. 'G-Mamma,' she muttered into her SPIV, 'I've found them.'

'On my way,' said G-Mamma indistinctly. 'Just testing the smoked salmon for . . . weevils. I mean, evils.'

Janey smiled and shook her head. Her SPI:KE would never change. 'Now, let's have a look,' she said, stepping forward to grab a box from the top of the pile.

But much to her surprise, Janey found that she was the one who was grabbed as two robotic claws reached out of the mince-pie tower and clamped her around the middle! Then they started to squeeze. 'Get off!' she gasped, batting at the pincers with her Girl-gauntlet. But the grip of the arms was too strong. The robotic claws were closing around her . . . she couldn't breathe . . . and for the second time that day the world was turning black . . .

mincemeat

Janey tried to rally her thoughts as the black cloud enveloped her. This could NOT be happening. A pile of pies was trying to make mincemeat of her. G-Mamma was on the way, but there could be a million tasty distractions between her and her Spylet. Janey wriggled fruitlessly. The pain across her middle was unbearable. She was being cut in half.

And that gave her an idea. The pincers were made of metal, and steel could definitely be cut. Grateful that her hands were free, Janey lifted her Girl-gauntlet and shot a laser beam straight into the monstrous claw. For a moment nothing happened, then several boxes of pies started to smoke, filling the air with a pungent Christmassy aroma. Janey held still for just a moment, and then the pincers began to melt. Janey grabbed one end of the pincer and yanked it from around her middle.

To her amazement there was a yelp of pain and a frantic rustling of the mince-pie boxes around her body, then the smouldering pie boxes collapsed in a heap. And there, buried among them, was a robotic arm, all bronze-coloured sinews and rivets.

G-Mamma now appeared from behind a display of Fondant Fancies. 'Blondey Blonde, could you draw *any* more attention to yourself?'

Janey was busy knocking pie boxes aside. 'I was attacked, G-Mamma. Something used these boxes to clamp me round the stomach and squash the life out of me. It must have been hiding behind them . . . ah!'

They both stared at the scene before them. There was no sign of a robotic monster, but there *was* a large hole in the pillar against which the pies had been stacked. It was about the size of the fireplace in Janey's bedroom . . . and Janey's Spylet instincts told her what she was looking at. She pressed the wall at the ten-past-

two position that activated her own spy-door –
and nodded as a white panel slid noiselessly into
place so that the pillar was just exactly that once
more. An ordinary pillar, in an ordinary department store. 'Yep,' she whispered. 'Spy-door.'

Suddenly the outraged Food Hall manager
rushed down the aisle towards them. 'Madam!
Young lady! What on earth are you doing?
You've ruined the whole display.'

Reaching for her basket, which already
held several items, including a half-eaten side
of smoked salmon and an empty bottle of
chocolate milk, G-Mamma grabbed armfuls
of the ribboned boxes and flung them in with
the shopping. 'Don't worry, I'm buying all of
these. Special favourite of mine, mince pies.
Yummety tummety yes indeedy.'

The manager walked off, bemused, and
Janey grabbed what was left of the robotic
arm. 'We'll have to check this out, G-Mamma.
Weird – it's much smaller than it felt when it
was squeezing me half to death . . .'

When they reached Winton School at one
thirty-one G-Mamma screeched to a halt and

Janey spotted Trouble waiting patiently for her at the gates. He had obviously treated himself to a Wower and was flicking his magnificent burnished tail to and fro. Together they made for the reception hut.

'Emma Bower ... Ryan Petersen ... Anna Merrick ... Oh Janey, you're here.' Mrs Halliday snapped the register shut. 'Now, class, Janey's just going to keep an eye on you for a little while, as I've got some important things to do. Be good. Remember: you are not to leave the classroom. And do keep your pets under control, Cassie and Emma.'

Janey ushered Trouble into the room as Mrs Halliday swept out. 'Hello again, class.'

'Your bump's gone,' observed one small girl, and, 'You've got pretty boots,' said another. 'Cool glasses,' remarked a boy.

Janey pulled her skirt down self-consciously. She'd forgotten she had her SPIsuit on underneath. 'Yes, I'm feeling much better. Let me introduce you to my pet. This is Trouble, my cat.'

The children called, 'Hello, Trouble,' and

crowded round to pat his quiffed head. He preened and stretched his neck, loving the attention.

'So, Emma, what pet have you got?' asked Janey.

Emma stood up from her desk carrying a bowl with a goldfish in it. The water slopped all over the teacher's desk as she put it down.

'He's called Jaws,' said Emma shyly.

'That's great, Emma,' said Janey. 'Now why don't we come and look at Jaws, one by one . . .'

Once the children had had enough of the goldfish, Janey turned her attention to Cassie. 'Let's see your pet now, shall we?'

Cassie blinked solemnly at Janey from behind her glasses. She looked rather like an animal herself, thought Janey – a bushbaby or a little marmoset. She hoisted a large cage on to her desk. 'I've brought Gerry.'

'Bring Gerry to the front then.'

Cassie stepped up to the desk, holding the cage as if it weighed nothing, and parked it on the teacher's table. 'I have lots of special pets, but Gerry the gerbil is my favourite.

He's very clever,' she said, opening the cage door and reaching in a hand.

Suddenly there was a flash of golden brown and Gerry leaped out of the cage. Instantly Trouble's fur stood on end.

'It's not a mouse!' yelled Janey, knowing how scared Trouble was of them. But it was too late. The gerbil – whose claws and teeth were rather sharp and long, Janey noticed – launched himself off the table and across the classroom. Trouble took off after him, and Janey dropped to the floor and lunged for Gerry but didn't even manage to touch him as he seemed to fly towards the door, which Mrs Halliday had left ajar. Suddenly pandemonium broke out and Gerry's cage was knocked off the table, landing on the back of Janey's head with a reverberating clang. And before she knew it, darkness fell again.

5 pies and spies

'Kids . . . uh . . . class . . .' Janey muttered a minute or two later, when she finally managed to open her eyes. She shoved the cage off her back, trying to ignore the sickly, lurching feeling in her stomach, possibly caused by the fact that the classroom, apart from a madly flapping goldfish that had been tipped out of its bowl on to the floor, was completely empty. 'Oh no.'

She clambered unsteadily to her feet, clutching the tabletop for support. The room was swaying badly – even when she sat down it still felt as though the walls were shifting from side to side. She went to rest her head in her hands but missed the table completely, dropping her elbows straight into her lap. 'Ow! Oh, this is worse than . . .'

Suddenly she looked up. She hadn't just missed the table. The table wasn't there. It had slid over to the right! Now it was sliding back towards her. Janey focused hazily on the other desks. They were all making the same motion, back and forth across the classroom as if they were on the deck of a ship caught in a storm.

It wasn't just her head that was rocking.

It was the whole room.

As steadily as she could Janey staggered to the door, stopping to scoop up Jaws and pop him back in his now half-empty bowl. The whole classroom was definitely moving, with desks colliding into her and pencils and rulers raining on to the floor. Janey tugged open the door and looked outside.

'What are you doing?!' Janey ran back inside and lurched from window to window of the hut, staring down. She could hardly believe her eyes.

Each of the twelve reception-class children was stationed outside at a particular point of the classroom hut – two at each corner, two at the back wall and one at the centre of each side wall. Beneath their little caps their faces were

pink and sweaty, but their expressions were grit-
tily determined. The receptioners were shifting
their classroom away from the main school, out
across the playing field and towards the woods.

Wrenching open the door, Janey waved her
hands. 'Stop! What are you doing? You know
you weren't meant to . . . to leave the classroom.'
As if *that* was the worst thing they were doing.

'We didn't leave the classroom,' said Cassie.
'We're taking it.'

'Why?'

Cassie let go of her side of the building
abruptly, and the whole classroom tipped to one
side. The other children didn't seem to be able to
hold it without her, so they all let go. The building thumped down on to the ground. 'It doesn't
matter *why*,' said Cassie, her long-lashed hazel
eyes the picture of innocence. 'We'll come back
in now, *Miss Janey* . . . Come on, class!'

Janey felt like she was in a very weird dream
as she stepped back and watched the class file
past her and straighten their desks. Emma, the
owner of Jaws the goldfish, looked dumbly at
the bowl as if she was in a trance.

'Did you find Gerry?' Janey suddenly

remembered when all the strange activity had begun.

Cassie turned to Janey. 'Of course I did,' she squeaked. 'As I said, he's a very *special* pet. Just like your Trouble.'

And as Cassie smiled, a cold hand closed around Janey's heart. A menacing tone had entered Cassie's voice. And what's more, Trouble was *special* for one particular reason. He was a spy-pet – no ordinary cat. And Gerry was no ordinary gerbil. Hadn't he been unnaturally fast, and hadn't he had what looked like *fangs*? Janey shuddered. Gerry was a spy-pet too. But a nasty one. And he belonged to someone nasty . . .

Suddenly the little smiling faces of the reception class turned to hideous leers, like rows of Halloween pumpkins. Led by one very strong five-year-old, they had carted their classroom out of sight of the school and trapped Janey inside. They might be small, but Jane Blonde was in very big trouble indeed.

Fumbling for her SPIV, Janey tried to ignore the piercing stares of the children surrounding her. 'G-Mamma,' she shouted feverishly, 'I've just worked it out. It's not *mince pies* we have to look out for. It's 'Min Spies'. Beware MinSpies. Dad was trying to warn us about *miniature spies*. And I'm surrounded by them.'

6 perspiring peril

Smiling sweetly and straightening her cap, Cassie advanced on Janey. 'You took your time, Blonde. You've been knocked out by a tree, half-squeezed to death by my very special Girl-gauntlets – one of which you kindly broke – and spynapped in a classroom while you were un-conscious. Weren't you even the teensiest bit suspicious?'

'Why would I suspect a bunch of toddlers?' Janey retreated behind the desk, away from Cassie. She could see the MinSpy's undam-aged metal glove glinting beneath her shirt cuff. 'What did you do with your teacher?'

'Just a little food poisoning. And then of course I put in my special request to get you here.'

'And you were in Seacrest and Argents?'

Cassie laughed, taking off her glasses to reveal eyes as flinty as an eagle's and only a tiny bit bigger. The magnifying lenses had made her look much more childlike. Now she just looked like a tiny adult, in spite of the school uniform – a tiny adult who was actually an enemy spy.

'Ah yes, the mince-pie attack. I did a little eavesdropping at the headmistress's door and decided to pop to the shops. I nearly had you, Blonde. You see, *my* Girl-gauntlet multiplies my arm strength by ten times. I'm much stronger than you, despite my size.' She reached over and flung the desk out of the way, straight over the heads of the rest of the class, who had all sat down on their cushions and were staring at the whiteboard as if awaiting instructions. The table smashed against the back wall, but none of the children – the MinSpies – so much as flinched.

Janey backed away again. Cassie pursued. Janey dodged. Cassie ducked. Janey was backed up against the little sink where the children washed their paintbrushes after they'd been doing art. Their paintings – swoops and swipes of broad colour with no obvious shape or design – were hanging from strings across the classroom. These spies must have been very busy pretending to be kids, thought Janey. Just as Cassie reached out for her, she sat back against the sink, planted her feet on the small spy's chest and pushed with all her might. The Fleet-feet impacted enough to send Cassie vaulting back across the room. In that moment, Janey grabbed the end of one of the painting garlands and jumped over to Cassie, wrapping her in a strange mummy-like encasing of paper and string.

'You can't stop me,' scoffed Cassie.

To Janey's horror, her enemy sat up straight, braced her arms against the string and pushed outwards. She was right – Janey might as well have tried to use a spider's web to stop a rhinoceros. In moments, Cassie was back on her feet, straightening her school cap and running towards Janey with an expression of such ferocity that Janey wondered how she could ever have thought she was *cute*.

She had to keep out of the way of those

murderous arms. The laser had worked before so, training her ring finger on Cassie's sleeves, Janey aimed and fired.

Cassie cried out, the same little yelp that Janey had heard in the department store, then lunged forward to grab her foe.

Instinctively Janey covered her throat, which was a mistake.

Cassie's vicious pincer formed a clamp around her arm. She couldn't move. She was completely helpless as Cassie lifted her straight above her head like a champion wrestler, preparing to drop her to the floor.

'Desks!' shouted Cassie. 'Now, class!'

At once the children shook themselves out of their strange trances. Each of them marched over to the nearest desk and, with considerable grunting and puffing, they piled the desks against each other.

'Move the cushions,' added Cassie. 'She is NOT to have a soft landing.'

Janey wriggled hopelessly as the children flung the cushions to the edges of the room. Cassie was going to throw her directly on to the pile of desks with such force that Janey would break her neck. It was strange that she was so strong she could hold up a Spylet twice her size while the other children had needed to pair up to move their tiny tables.

'Spread out!' commanded Cassie, easing her grip on Janey for one second, just long enough to straighten her cap again. 'There'll be big splinters – no need for any of you to get hurt . . . yet.'

The threat in her words was obvious, but why were all the children listening to her? wondered Janey.

'Come on, class,' she pleaded. 'You know I'm the teacher. You do what *Miss Janey* says, remember?' But the children stared at her blankly. It was hard to believe they were the same set of kids as the Snufflebug lovers.

Because . . . Janey could hardly stop herself from grinning triumphantly as the realization hit her . . . they *weren't* the same children. Not really. They were being brainwashed, manipulated by one evil MinSpy. The question was – how? She looked at all the stern little faces peeking out from under their school caps, and the answer occurred to her at once. 'X-ray,' she said softly to her Ultra-gogs, staring straight down at the top of Cassie's head.

And there it was. A tiny motherboard the size of an ant. 'They're wearing PERSPIREs!' Janey whispered. Cassie must have adjusted the hard drives so that she could use the computers to control the children's brains.

Janey quickly realized that the hats were her way out. If she could break Cassie's link to her own little army, Jane Blonde might just be able to stand up to the MinSpy. It was just a matter of discovering how to do that before it was too late.

claws and caws

'Your time is UP!' screeched Cassie, reaching back with her super-strong arm, ready to propel Janey into the pile of desks. 'Maximum impact – maximum damage.'

'Say bye to Miss Janey.'

As the children obediently repeated, 'Bye, Miss Janey,' the MinSpy launched Janey at breakneck speed across the classroom. As the Spylet flew towards the target she prepared to use the number-one tool in her spy kit. Soaring above the mountain of desks, Janey circled her head, whipping her blonde ponytail around the light fitting in the middle of the room. She caught hold of the end of her ponytail, and found herself suspended from the light, her feet dangling above the highest desk in the pile.

'No!' roared Cassie, almost spitting with fury as she started to climb the slipping, precarious pile of desks. 'You'd better prepare yourself – Gerry's feeling very peckish today!'

Janey looked on in horror as the fanged gerbil poked his head out of Cassie's blazer pocket. His eyes gleamed red and saliva dripped from his razor-sharp teeth.

She knew that they'd be on her in no time and that between Cassie's evil pincer arm and Gerry's fangs she would have no chance. The rest of the children were all watching, flat-eyed and disinterested. Janey needed *her* spy-pet now more than ever. 'Trouble, help!' she screamed as a wave of pain seared her scalp. 'Trouble!'

But it wasn't Trouble who appeared first – it was Maggie! Last seen sulking in G-Mamma's Spylab, Maggie was now fluttering at the classroom window, diving at it again and again but unable to get through. Janey had saved Maggie – and now Maggie was trying to save Janey! The bird flitted from window to window, but none was open. Jane gasped as a second rescuer came into view. Trouble had leaped on to the windowsill beneath Maggie!

53

'Trouble, sabre-claw,' screamed Janey.

Hearing his mistress, Trouble flicked out his cutlass-shaped claw and swiped across the glass. He then hooked his claw delicately around his handiwork and less than a second later a neat square of glass fell out on to the ground below.

As the cat leaped through the window, Janey had an idea.

'Maggie,' cried Janey. 'Maggie, she's controlling them via the caps! The PERSPIREs!'

Cawing excitedly, Maggie flew over Emma's head, swooped down and plucked the cap off the little girl's head. As Emma shook herself and looked around in bewilderment Maggie dropped the cap and moved on to the next child. And just as a screeching Cassie reached the top of the desk pile, all the hats had been removed. The children surveyed the chaos all around them, their eyes round with amazement. A few started blubbing as they realized they might actually be in serious trouble.

'That won't stop me, Blonde.'

Gerry jumped to nip at Janey's feet, and Cassie stretched out with her pincer. But Janey swung her leg out of the way just in time.

It was time for Jane Blonde to take charge.

'Children, listen to me,' she shouted. Eleven little human heads and two animal ones snapped back to look at her. 'Mrs Halliday's going to be very unhappy at the state of this classroom. Put the desks back now, please.'

And the children couldn't do it fast enough, running over to yank the desks out from the bottom of the pile. As the lower desks were removed the pile began to teeter, and suddenly, in a landslide of wood, chalk and poster paints, the whole construction tumbled to the floor. Cassie slithered down with it, helpless, and found herself on the floor, imprisoned in a cage of desk legs. Janey unlooped her ponytail and dropped neatly down from the light.

Maggie hovered threateningly over Gerry, and Trouble guarded Cassie, his sabre-claw winking in her face.

Janey turned her attention to the snivelling children. 'Don't worry, reception class. I'll have a word with the headmistress and everything will be OK. But Cassie's sick, and she has to go home.'

Janey pulled out her SPIV. The children

wouldn't remember anything after a little brain-wiping had been applied, but they still needed looking after while she handed the MinSpy over to SPI. 'G-Mamma, are you there?'

G-Mamma's face had a definite green tinge to it. 'Here, Blonde. Glad you found out about the MinSpy. I'd got sick of eating the actual mince pies.'

'Janey, where are you?' Mrs Halliday's face poked up next to G-Mamma's. 'We appear to have lost your classroom.'

Janey grinned. 'You'd better all come over to the lower field. And tell Alfie . . . there's a little bit more babysitting for him to do.'

There was a loud groan, which made Janey laugh. Her SPI team were obviously all together, awaiting her next move.

Who needed PERSPIREs to take control? she thought with a grin. Sometimes it was enough just to be Jane Blonde, the Perfect Spylet.

one hundred lucky winners will each receive an ultimate master spy kit to become a perfect spylet like jane blonde!

To enter, log on to **www.meetjaneblonde.com** or send a postcard with your name, age, address and an answer to the following question:

what is jane blonde's real name?
a) jane black
b) janine blonde
c) janey brown

Send your entry to:
World Book Day Jane Blonde Competition
Marketing Department
Macmillan Children's Books
20 New Wharf Road
London N1 9RR

for super spy tips, spytacular screensavers and to join the spy academy, visit www.meetjaneblonde.com